The Story of London

On line from River to Capital City

by Christopher Maynard
& Jacqui Bailey

A & C Black • London

Created for A & C Black Publishers Ltd. by Two's Company

Designed by Matthew Lilly

Illustrations by Katherine Baxter; David Cuzik (Pennant Illustration Agency); Tony Kenyon (B L Kearley); Matthew Lilly; Peter Visscher

Cover illustrations by Katharine Baxter (scenes); Clive Goodyear (Pennant Illustration Agency) (figures)

Reprinted 2003
First published in 2000 by A & C Black Publishers Limited,
37 Soho Square, London W1D 3QZ
www.acblack.com
in association with The London String of Pearls

A & C Black uses paper produced with elemental chlorine-free pulp, harvested from managed sustainable forests.

ISBN 0-7136-5386-8

Printed in Belgium
by Proost International Book Production

The Publishers would also like to thank the following for permission to use their photographs: Dylan Hammond (p14); London Transport Museum (p26); Lord Mayor's Coach Courtesy of the Corporation of London (p19b); Mission Management (p23); Museum of London (pp21, 25, 29); QA Photos (p31); Royal Collection Enterprises, Buckingham Palace © Her Majesty Queen Elizabeth II (p7); The London String of Pearls Millennium Festival (pp1, 6, 7, 9, 10, 11, 12, 15, 19t, 27).

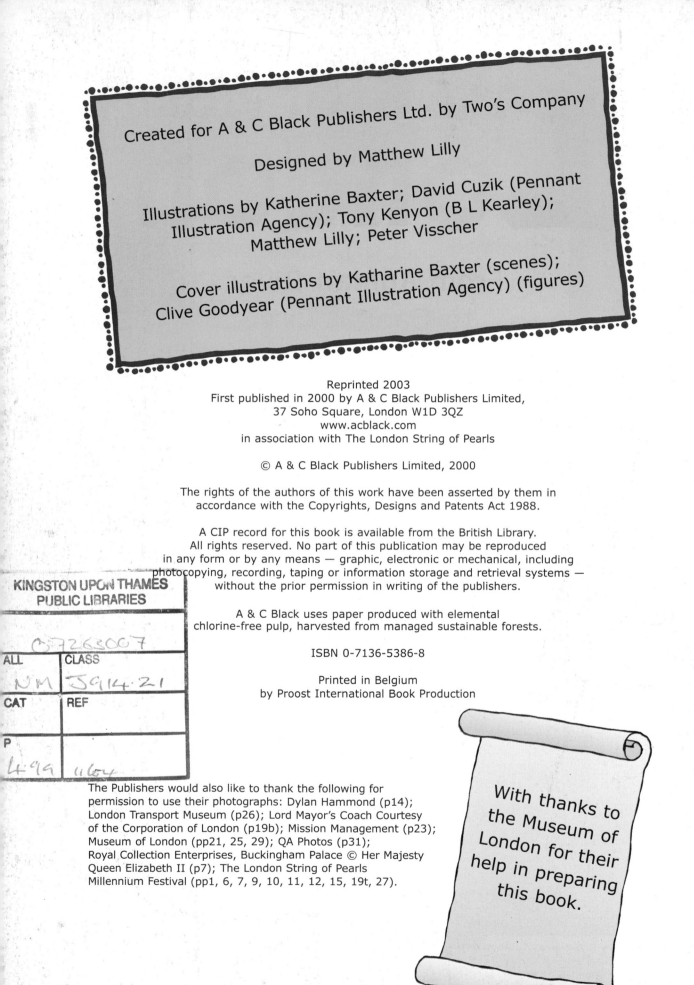

With thanks to the Museum of London for their help in preparing this book.

Contents

The First 1,000 Years

Way back, as far as anyone knows, people have lived in the London area. But they were hunters and farmers, so there was never a town here — until the Romans invaded.

London Bridge has been rebuilt at least four times since Roman days. The present bridge was put up in 1973.

Empire builders

In AD 43, the Romans landed in Britain. They conquered the British tribes in the south, and set about building forts and roads, then towns. The Romans knew it was important to control a crossing point at the River Thames, so they decided to build a settlement on the north bank. They chose a spot where the land rose in two small hills and where the river became narrower.

Roman soldiers were forever marching back and forth across the country — and wherever they went, supply carts followed. A bridge across the Thames was vital to them because it linked their ports on the south-east coast with the rest of Britain.

By AD 200, *Londinium* had a wall to protect it. It was over 3 kilometres long and as high as four men. At various points there were gates where paved roads led to other parts of the country.

Chunks of the wall can still be seen near Tower Hill, and some of the City's street names have the word 'gate' in them. To Londoners, 'the City' usually means just the part of London that was once surrounded by the Roman wall.

ROMAN ROAD

CRIPPLEGATE

BISHOPSGATE

NEWGATE

RIVER FLEET

L O N D I N I U M

ALDGATE

LUDGATE

ROMAN WALL

R I V E R   T H A M E S

BRIDGE

NORTH

750,000 YEARS AGO THE THAMES STARTS TO FLOW ON ITS PRESENT COURSE

500,000 YEARS AGO EARLY HUMANS ARE LIVING IN THE LONDON AREA

100 BC CELTIC TRIBES LIVE AROUND HEATHROW

The Romans laid out buildings, streets and a port, and shortly afterwards they built a bridge. They called the settlement *Londinium*.

A useful crossing

The first Roman bridge across the Thames was probably a row of boats tied side by side and covered with planks. Later, a solid wooden roadway was laid on top of columns sunk deep into the river bed.

A network of paved roads connected this river crossing with other important towns to the north and east. From the south side of the bridge, roads led to the coastal ports that linked Britain to the rest of the Roman Empire.

ROAD
BUILDER
AT
WORK

Rise and fall

Within 20 years, the settlement had become a bustling town of 20,000 people and the most important centre in Britain.

London thrived under the Romans, but when the Roman Empire collapsed the good times came to an end.

In AD 410 the Romans left Britain and, just 40 years later, London was a ghost town.

Over the next 600 years, Britain was invaded again and again — this time by warlike tribes from northern Europe.

By the AD 700s, London had become a small trading settlement again, and in the 890s King Alfred the Great resettled it as a town.

All Fall Down

Between about AD 800 and 1016, London was attacked a number of times by Vikings.

In 1014, Danish Vikings had taken over London and the Saxon king asked King Olaf of Norway to help him get it back. During the battle, King Olaf is said to have tied ropes from his boats to the posts beneath London Bridge and pulled it (and the Danes) into the river.

AD 43
ROMAN ARMIES
ARRIVE IN
BRITAIN

AD 50s
THE ROMANS
BEGIN TO BUILD
LONDINIUM

AD 410
THE LAST ROMAN
SOLDIERS LEAVE
BRITAIN

A Royal Home

Because of its port and bridge London was an important town, but it wasn't the country's capital. Kings of the time moved around so much that there was no capital city.

Things began to change in 1050, though, when King Edward the Confessor started to build a great church, called **WESTMINSTER ABBEY**, about 3 kilometres west of London, beyond a bend of the Thames.

So that he could keep a close eye on the building work, Edward also built a new home between the abbey and the river. It was called the **PALACE OF WESTMINSTER**, and by moving there, along with all of his servants, advisers and other members of the royal court, Edward took the first step towards making London the country's capital city.

King Henry III tore down Edward's abbey in the 1200s and began building the church we see today. It took nearly 300 years to finish it.

Since William the Conqueror was crowned in Westminster Abbey in 1066, all English kings and queens except for two have been crowned there.

Westminster Abbey was so important to Edward that he watched over its construction himself. It was finished in 1065, just in time for Christmas. A week later, Edward died and was buried there.

1050 WORK BEGINS ON WESTMINSTER ABBEY.

1066 WILLIAM THE CONQUEROR WINS THE BATTLE OF HASTINGS

ABOUT 1070 WILLIAM BUILDS THE TOWER OF LONDON

Home from home

Kings and their courts went on moving about a lot, but the Palace of Westminster remained a royal home until 1547, when Henry VIII moved to Whitehall Palace. Henry had itchy feet and owned more than 60 grand houses around the country. If he liked a place, he simply begged, bought or stole it!

When Charles II became king in 1660, though, he decided that he'd rather live in **ST JAMES'S PALACE** nearby.

Nearly two hundred years later, in the 1820s, King George IV took a fancy to a large mansion that his father had bought, called Buckingham House. George rebuilt it in a much grander style and called it **BUCKINGHAM PALACE**.

Buckingham Palace has been the main royal home for about 180 years now — it must be nearly time for another royal move!

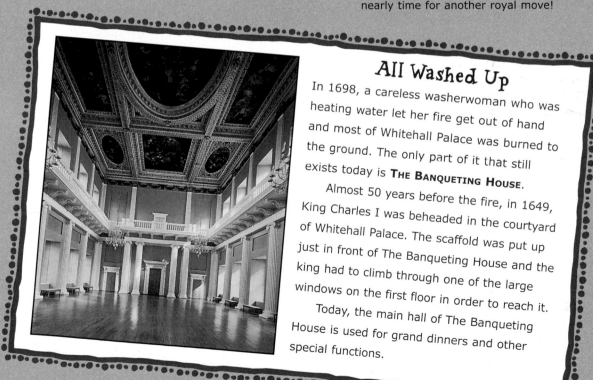

All Washed Up

In 1698, a careless washerwoman who was heating water let her fire get out of hand and most of Whitehall Palace was burned to the ground. The only part of it that still exists today is **THE BANQUETING HOUSE**.

Almost 50 years before the fire, in 1649, King Charles I was beheaded in the courtyard of Whitehall Palace. The scaffold was put up just in front of The Banqueting House and the king had to climb through one of the large windows on the first floor in order to reach it.

Today, the main hall of The Banqueting House is used for grand dinners and other special functions.

GUESS WHAT? How many kings and queens have been crowned in Westminster Abbey? a) 18 b) 38 c) 108

1193
HENRY FITZAILWIN BECOMES THE CITY OF LONDON'S FIRST MAYOR

1209
THE FIRST STONE LONDON BRIDGE IS BUILT

1269
THE REBUILDING OF WESTMINSTER ABBEY BEGINS

Palace to Parliament

The word 'parliament' comes from a French word that means 'to talk'.

In the Middle Ages, the king made all the decisions about how to rule the country. Sometimes he held meetings with a group of his most powerful lords and bishops, who advised him on the laws he made. These meetings were called Parliaments and, over the years, they became more and more important.

The number of advisers grew until, in the mid-1300s, Parliament divided into two groups, called the House of Commons and the House of Lords.

Members of the House of Commons were elected (voted for) by wealthy merchants and landowners. Members of the House of Lords were nobles and bishops chosen by the king.

Treason and Plot

People didn't always agree with the king. In 1605, a group of rebels came up with a fiendish plot to blow up King James I and the members of his Parliament.

Trust me, the plan is foolproof!

The rebels filled a cellar in the Palace of Westminster with barrels of gunpowder. One of the plotters, Guy Fawkes, was to set off the explosion on November 5th, while the King and Parliament were meeting.

They'll never know what hit 'em.

But the gunpowder was discovered and all the plotters, including Guy Fawkes, were hanged for treason. Every year since then, on November 5th, people remember the 'Gunpowder Plot' by letting off fireworks and burning dummies of Guy on bonfires.

Moving around

The Commons held meetings in Westminster Abbey, while the Lords met in the Palace of Westminster. But when Henry VIII moved out of the palace in 1547, the Commons moved in and began meeting there, too.

Today, Parliament rules the country, rather than the king or queen, and the Palace of Westminster is usually called the **HOUSES OF PARLIAMENT**.

1348
PLAGUE KILLS
ONE THIRD OF ALL
LONDONERS

1391–1419
DICK WHITTINGTON
IS MAYOR OF
LONDON

1535–1539
HENRY VIII SELLS
MONASTERY
LANDS

A Big Bell

The Palace of Westminster burned down in 1834, after a heating stove set some wood panelling ablaze.

When the palace was rebuilt, new bells were hung in the clock tower. The biggest bell is known as Big Ben and — though nobody knows for sure — most people think it was named after the large Welshman, Benjamin Hall, who was put in charge of the new clock tower.

Big Ben weighs 13.5 tonnes (more than 12 cars) and is over 2 metres tall.

Commons rule

Nowadays, members of the House of Commons (called MPs) are elected by all the British people. There are more than 650 MPs and they belong to different groups or 'parties'.

The party with the most MPs forms the government, and that party's leader becomes the head of the government — the Prime Minister.

Members of the House of Lords still aren't elected, but these days they're chosen by the Prime Minister. The Lords cannot govern the country, but they can delay laws from being made. However, it is the Prime Minister and his or her government who make the final decisions by voting.

When Parliament is meeting, a light shines from Big Ben's clock tower at night and by day a flag flies from Victoria Tower at the other end of the building.

1547
HENRY VIII
DIES

1576
LONDON'S FIRST
THEATRE OPENS

1599
THE ORIGINAL
GLOBE THEATRE
IS BUILT

City of Churches

Churches were at the centre of people's lives in the Middle Ages. People went to church to hear mass, to pray, and to find comfort from the worries of life.

London had plenty of religious houses, too. These were monasteries and convents where monks and nuns lived and worked.

Most religious houses gave food and shelter to the poor and homeless. Some of them cared for the sick as well (they were the only places that did). Today, **St Thomas' Hospital** is a vast, modern building, but in the 1100s it was part of a monastery.

There were 126 parish churches in the City of London in the 1300s. The noise of their bells ringing must have been deafening!

Burned, Bombed, but still There

There has been a **St Paul's Cathedral** in London for 1400 years. The building we see today is the sixth cathedral. Most of the earlier ones burned down. This St Paul's was finished in 1711, and so far it's been lucky. In spite of being hit by bombs in World War II, it's still standing.

The huge 111-metre dome of St Paul's is one of the most famous sights in London. From the Golden Gallery that runs around it, there's a stupendous view of London. Over three million people climb the 650 steps up to the Gallery every year.

1600
LONDON'S POPULATION GROWS TO 200,000 PEOPLE

1603
ELIZABETH I DIES AT RICHMOND

1632
THE FIRST BUILDINGS GO UP AT COVENT GARDEN

Power at the top

The people who ran the Church were usually rich and powerful noblemen, who were given their jobs by the Pope — the head of the Church in Rome. As well as advising the king, they made sure that the churches and monasteries were taking proper care of people's religious needs. They also spent a lot of time having more churches built.

Priests and clerics were less important, but unlike most people they knew how to read and write. They often ran the law courts and other government offices.

LAMBETH PALACE has been the London home of the Archbishops of Canterbury since 1197. Today, the Queen is head of the Church of England, but the Archbishop of Canterbury is its spiritual leader.

Royalty takes over

In the 1530s, however, King Henry VIII quarrelled with the Pope and made himself head of the Church of England. The enormous wealth of the monasteries was too great a temptation for Henry. Before long, he closed them all down and declared that their lands and wealth belonged to him.

In London, Henry sold off most of this land and soon streets and houses were springing up where monastery buildings and gardens had once been.

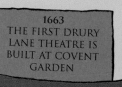

Land for Sale

1637
THE FIRST ROYAL PARK, HYDE PARK, IS OPENED TO THE PUBLIC

1649
KING CHARLES I IS BEHEADED AT WHITEHALL PALACE

1663
THE FIRST DRURY LANE THEATRE IS BUILT AT COVENT GARDEN

Crime and Punishment

Public hangings took place on a gallows called 'Tyburn Tree'. Today, a stone near MARBLE ARCH marks where the gallows once stood.

If you sold rotten meat in the City of London in the 1500s, you were dragged through the streets with the meat hung around your neck. More serious crimes, like fighting, might lead to paying a fine or being flung in prison. Thieves and murderers were hanged.

By the 1700s, more and more hangings were taking place — even for as little as stealing a loaf of bread. London had grown, and more people meant more crime. There was no police force to keep people in order. The government hoped that the threat of hanging would do the trick — but it didn't.

Tower Power

The **TOWER OF LONDON** was both a palace and a terrifying prison. William the Conqueror built the stone fortress, known as the White Tower, in the 1070s. The outer walls and moat were added later.

William put the Tower inside the City to warn rebellious Londoners to stay loyal to him. Other rulers used it for keeping enemies of the crown under control as well. Many of the noble guests who were sent there never left it alive!

Today, the Tower houses a great collection of royal armour and the Crown Jewels. You can also visit the spot where favoured prisoners were beheaded in private — away from the jeering crowds at the public executions on Tower Hill.

1665
PLAGUE STRIKES LONDON FOR THE LAST TIME

1666
THE GREAT FIRE OF LONDON BURNS FOR FIVE DAYS

1671
COLONEL BLOOD TRIES TO STEAL THE CROWN JEWELS FROM THE TOWER

The arm of the law

In the 1750s, two London magistrates (judges) set up a group of detectives, known as the Bow Street Runners, to hunt down crooks for Bow Street Magistrates Court.

A similar group patrolled the River Thames in 1800, but neither of them made much difference to everyday crime.

Then, in 1829, a member of the government called Sir Robert Peel came up with a better idea. He set up the Metropolitan Police Force.

It was the first trained police force in the country and it was so successful that others soon followed.

Robert Peel's policemen were nicknamed 'bobbies' or 'peelers', after his name. They wore uniforms and carried short wooden clubs called truncheons.

Daylight Robbery!

Highwaymen were common on the roads into London. But though they stole travellers' money and jewellery they did not usually harm anyone. Sometimes a highwayman would become famous, such as Jack Shepperd. When he was caught and hanged in 1724, more than 80,000 people showed up to cheer and groan, as they watched him die at the end of a rope.

Dishing out justice

Small crimes, such as fighting, were tried in local magistrates courts (just as they are today). Cases of serious theft and murder were dealt with in higher courts. The main criminal court was (and still is) the **OLD BAILEY**. But people aren't hanged for murder or theft any longer. If they're found guilty they are sent to prison, sometimes for the rest of their life.

Complicated or important cases are sent to the High Court at the **ROYAL COURTS OF JUSTICE**. Until 1882, the High Court shared Westminster Palace with Parliament. Then it moved to the Royal Courts in the Strand, where it is today.

1694
THE BANK OF ENGLAND OPENS IN CHEAPSIDE

1698
MOST OF WHITEHALL PALACE BURNS DOWN

1711
THE PRESENT ST PAUL'S IS FINISHED

A River Highway

Ships of all kinds packed the River Thames in the 1700s. About half of them carried coal from the north-east of England to heat the City.

London's fame and fortune is due to one thing — its river. All through the Middle Ages the Thames was one of London's main highways. Barges and river boats brought fish, wood and wool to the City, while hundreds of watermen in small rowing boats ferried people up and down.

By the 1700s, trading ships were arriving with every tide, carrying all kinds of goods for sale in the City. Tea, silk and a fortune in spices came from the East. Sugar was brought from the Caribbean, timber from Norway and iron ore from Sweden.

The Thames was so busy that traffic on the river could barely move. Sometimes, dozens of ships queued up for days along the banks, waiting to get to a dock to unload.

Before trading ships could unload, they had to stop at the Custom House so the king's officials could decide how much tax had to be paid on their cargo. Today, London still has a **CUSTOM HOUSE** by the Thames, where Customs and Excise officers work to catch smugglers.

1740
SADLER'S WELLS
THEATRE IS
BUILT

1750
LONDON'S
SECOND BRIDGE,
WESTMINSTER
BRIDGE, OPENS

1753
MANSION HOUSE
BECOMES THE OFFICIAL
HOME OF LONDON'S
LORD MAYOR

Locked In

ST KATHARINE DOCK is a deep pool linked to the Thames by lock gates. Built in 1825, it was once filled with trading ships loading and unloading their cargoes and taking on fresh supplies.

Today, the dock is a busy marina where yachts and motor boats float alongside a collection of old ships — a lightship, a coastal steamer, a tug and a Thames barge.

In the dock

The delay in getting hold of their goods drove City merchants wild with frustration. Eventually, to ease the jam, a great sprawl of new docks and warehouses was built to the east of the City in the early 1800s, in the area known as the East End. The docks were given names like West India Dock and Russia Dock, which said much about where the ships that used them came from.

The ships, the docks and the warehouses all provided jobs, so workers flooded into the East End. Most of them came from other parts of the country, but some came from abroad, too.

Today the docks are mostly empty and the warehouses are being rebuilt as homes. Big ships no longer come so far upriver. Instead, yachts and tour boats cruise the Thames.

In the 1600s, the Thames sometimes froze over and Frost Fairs were held on the ice with stalls, puppet shows and football games. It was even possible to drive a coach and horses along the river.

1761
KING GEORGE III
BUYS BUCKINGHAM
HOUSE

1769
BLACKFRIARS
BRIDGE IS
BUILT

1787
THE ORIGINAL
LORD'S CRICKET
GROUND OPENS

15

Bridging the Gap

For 1,700 years, there was only one bridge across the Thames at London. When a stone bridge replaced the wooden one in 1209, homes and workshops sprouted all along it until the central lane was just 4 metres wide.

The lane became so clogged with carts, animals and people that at times it was impossible to get across.

At last, in 1750, a second bridge was put up. It crossed the river at Westminster, replacing the ancient ferry at Lambeth that had taken people across. A few years after that, Blackfriars Bridge was built near Fleet Street.

Suddenly there were bridges springing up everywhere. From 1800 to 1819, three bridges were built — at Vauxhall, Waterloo and Southwark. And, as it became easier to get from one side to the other, more and more people went to live south of the river.

In 1733, all traffic on London Bridge was ordered to 'keep to the left'. In time, this became the rule of the road, which is why we drive on the left today.

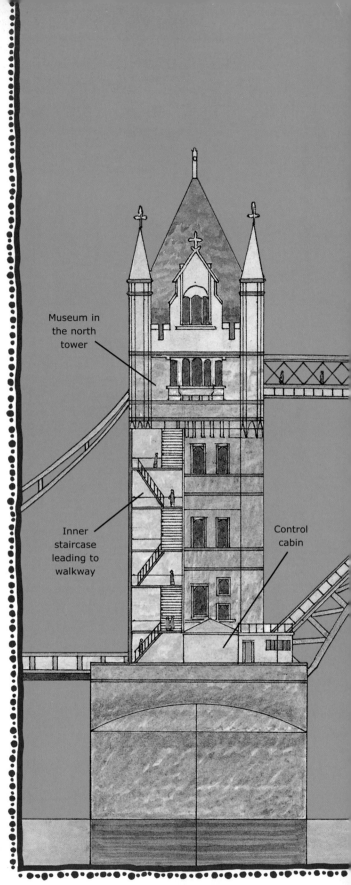

Museum in the north tower

Inner staircase leading to walkway

Control cabin

1801
LONDON'S POPULATION RISES TO JUST UNDER 1 MILLION

1809
THE FIRST GAS STREET LIGHTING IS USED IN PALL MALL

1814
GAS STREET LIGHTING IS INSTALLED IN PICCADILLY

In the Swing

The last major road bridge to be built over the River Thames
became the most famous one of all. Tower Bridge was put up
in 1894, when large trading ships still came upriver to unload.
The only way the ships could get past the new bridge was if
the roadway divided in two and lifted up to let them through.

Towers were built to house the giant machinery and the
counterweights needed to swing up the two halves. A walkway
was hung above the road so that people could still cross over
when the bridge was raised.

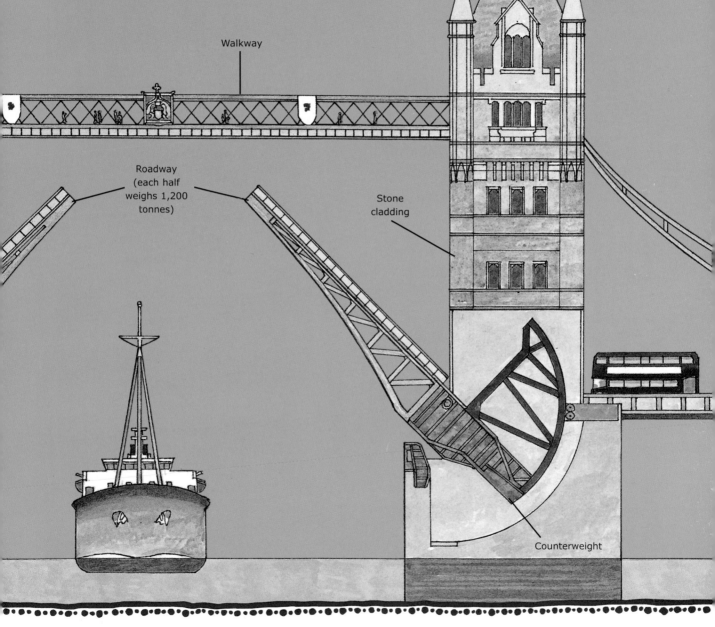

Walkway

Roadway
(each half
weighs 1,200
tonnes)

Stone
cladding

Counterweight

1816
VAUXHALL
BRIDGE OPENS

1817
WATERLOO
BRIDGE OPENS

1819
SOUTHWARK
BRIDGE OPENS

City of Gold

F or hundreds of years, the City of London has been one of the great trading centres of the world. Almost from the start, merchants and craftsmen clustered around its port like bees around a honeypot.

Clubbing together

I n the Middle Ages, these traders formed groups called guilds. Each guild specialised in one business. The Drapers traded in cloth, the Fishmongers in fish, the Goldsmiths in gold and silver, and so on.

By the 1400s, there were almost a hundred different guilds in the City. It was hard to carry out any trade without joining one of them. Those who tried often found themselves forced out of the City.

The guilds competed so fiercely with each other that the boys who worked for them often fought one another in the streets.

Turn Again, Whittington

The City of London's most famous mayor is Dick Whittington. Legend has it that Dick came to London as a penniless young man to seek his fortune.

He failed, but as he was leaving the church bells of the City told him to turn back and he would become mayor. Dick did so and, sure enough, he did become mayor — not just once but four times between 1391 and 1419.

1829
FIRST HORSE-DRAWN BUS SERVICE FROM PADDINGTON TO BANK

1829
THE METROPOLITAN POLICE FORCE IS SET UP BY ROBERT PEEL

1831
A NEW LONDON BRIDGE IS PUT UP (IT WAS SOLD TO AMERICA IN 1969)

Lord of the City

In time, the guilds were so wealthy they more or less ran the City.

The City of London had (and still has) its own laws and the right to govern itself. The job of governing it was done by a mayor. Every year a new mayor was chosen by the twelve most powerful guilds — often from among their own members.

By the end of the 1400s, the job was so important that people began using the title 'Lord Mayor', even though few of the mayors were noblemen.

In the money

Today, City of London traders are still famous for buying and selling. These days, though, they mostly buy and sell shares in other people's businesses.

Members of the Goldsmiths' Guild helped to invent banking in the 1600s. This guild was so rich and powerful it had its own lavish hall for its members to meet in. There is still a **GOLDSMITHS' HALL** in use today.

The City also has hundreds of banks and insurance companies, including the Bank of England, which handles all the government's money. Billions and billions of pounds pass through the City every day.

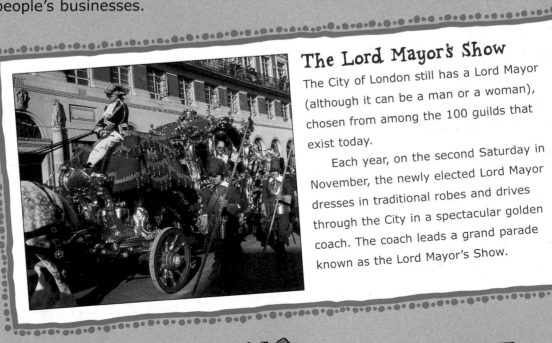

The Lord Mayor's Show

The City of London still has a Lord Mayor (although it can be a man or a woman), chosen from among the 100 guilds that exist today.

Each year, on the second Saturday in November, the newly elected Lord Mayor dresses in traditional robes and drives through the City in a spectacular golden coach. The coach leads a grand parade known as the Lord Mayor's Show.

1834
THE PALACE OF WESTMINSTER BURNS DOWN

1836
FIRST PASSENGER RAILWAY OPENS, FROM THE CITY TO GREENWICH

1838
THE NATIONAL GALLERY OPENS ITS DOORS

Death and Disaster

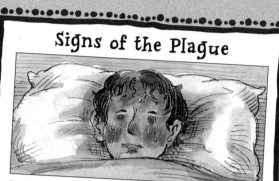

Just as in any city where people are crowded together, Londoners had their share of diseases. Nothing had prepared them for the horrors of the plague, though.

It broke out for the first time in 1348, when flea-ridden rats came ashore from cargo ships. No one realised that the fleas carried the disease, and once they began biting people the plague spread like wildfire. Before long, up to 200 people were dying each day.

The plague of 1665 killed one in four Londoners, perhaps as many as 60,000 people in all.

Plague city

For the next 300 years the plague returned again and again. The outbreak we know most about was in 1665, because the writer Samuel Pepys described it in his diary.

It broke out in February and by June the wealthy had fled to the safety of the countryside. In July alone, 6,000 Londoners died.

The next two months were even worse. Houses with plague victims inside had to be locked up. The doors could only be opened at night to take out corpses for burying.

That September, Pepys wrote that the once-crowded streets were all but empty. Finally, by Christmas, the plague came to an end.

Signs of the Plague

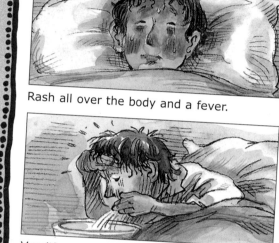

Rash all over the body and a fever.

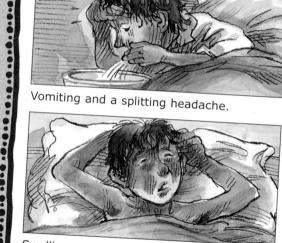

Vomiting and a splitting headache.

Swellings under the arms and in the groin which turn black.

Death in as little as two days.

1838
EUSTON AND PADDINGTON STATIONS OPEN

1841
TRAFALGAR SQUARE IS LAID OUT

1843
THE FIRST RAILWAY TUNNEL IS DUG UNDER THE THAMES

The Great Fire destroyed 13,200 houses, 89 churches and 400 streets.

A baker's oven

The following year, in 1666, a baker in Pudding Lane, close to London Bridge, was busy making bread. In the early hours of the morning of Sunday September 2nd, sparks from his oven set his house on fire. The flames spread and before long the whole neighbourhood was ablaze.

The fire spread to the warehouses along the river where it became a roaring inferno. By Monday the flames were leaping across whole streets at a time. People who were 48 kilometres away were showered with ash. The next day, old St Paul's Cathedral began to burn and molten lead from its roof rained down on to the nearby streets.

At last, on Wednesday, the blaze burned itself out. By Friday the fire was over. Within its walls, the City that had flourished all through the Middle Ages was a smoking ruin.

THE MONUMENT is a 65-metre-high tower that was built in memory of the fire. There are stairs inside it which you can climb to look out over the City.

1843
NELSON'S COLUMN
IS PUT UP IN
TRAFALGAR SQUARE

1847
THE BRITISH
MUSEUM MOVES
TO ITS PRESENT
HOME

1848
WATERLOO
STATION
OPENS

The Great Sprawl

In the 1600s, the area between the City of Westminster and the City of London became known as the 'West End'.

Throughout the Middle Ages most of London crowded within its city walls, while the village of Westminster grew into a town and then a city. But when London finally did burst out, it swamped the surrounding countryside.

Filling in the gaps

Long before the Great Fire, a string of mansions lay along the Thames between the City of London and the City of Westminster. The mansions belonged to wealthy nobles who regularly left their country homes to visit the royal court. In the 1600s, people began building on the old monastery lands and farmlands that lay behind these mansions.

In the rush to rebuild the City after the Great Fire, Londoners soon found that they needed more space. Before long, new roads and houses were springing up everywhere on the north side of the Thames, and the boundary between the cities of London and Westminster became blurred.

In the 1000s, London was pretty much the same size as the old Roman walled city.

By the end of the 1600s, the City of London and the City of Westminster had joined up to become one city.

By 1900, London had spread in all directions, swamping the villages and towns around it. (Today, London is so big that it cannot all fit on to this map.)

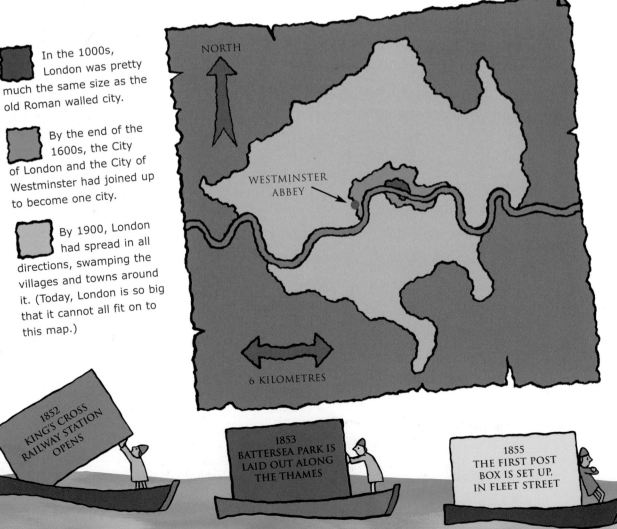

NORTH

WESTMINSTER ABBEY

6 KILOMETRES

1852
KING'S CROSS
RAILWAY STATION
OPENS

1853
BATTERSEA PARK IS
LAID OUT ALONG
THE THAMES

1855
THE FIRST POST
BOX IS SET UP,
IN FLEET STREET

A Growing Garden

COVENT GARDEN, in the West End, was once a vegetable garden belonging to Westminster Abbey. In 1632, the Earl of Bedford built a house here, with a large square in front of it called the Piazza. Before long, a fruit and vegetable market sprang up in the Piazza.

By the 1830s, the market at Covent Garden had become one of the biggest in London. In 1974, the market moved across the river, and today the Piazza is full of shops, cafés and street theatre.

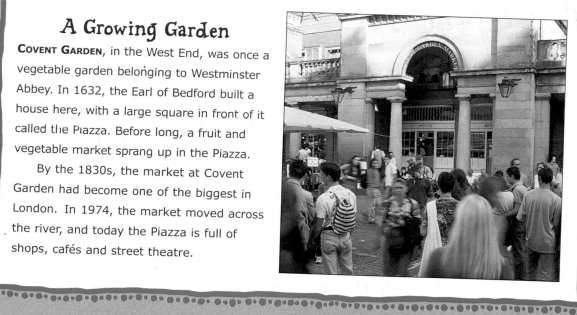

Spreading out

London's population grew from half a million in 1700 to almost a million in 1800. Much of this growth was due to newcomers looking for work. Few of them had any money, so they settled where the rents were lowest — to the east of the City, and in parts of the West End.

For a while the river remained a barrier to the south. But when the bridges went up at Westminster and then Blackfriars it was like pulling the cork from a bottle. A steady flow of people headed for the other side and, by 1801, one in six Londoners was living south of the river.

Once the railways arrived in the 1830s, there was no limit to London's growth. Now people could go to work in the City but live far outside it, where there was plenty of room and fresh air.

People who were too poor to move out of London had to live where they could walk to work. By the 1870s, many people were crowding into rows of cheap houses in the East End. Often, several families lived in each house, sharing one toilet and kitchen.

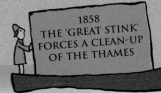

1858
THE 'GREAT STINK' FORCES A CLEAN-UP OF THE THAMES

1860
VICTORIA STATION OPENS

1861
GOVERNMENT OFFICES MOVE TO BUILDINGS ALONG WHITEHALL

The Great Stink

Between July and October, in 1849, one outbreak of cholera killed 14,000 Londoners.

After 1665 the plague never returned to London, but the city faced other problems. Polluted water and then polluted air killed Londoners by the thousand.

Loads of rubbish

For hundreds of years people simply left their rubbish to rot in the street until the rain or road sweepers cleared it away. Or they tossed it into the Thames. Almost everything ended up in the Thames — household waste, factory chemicals, even dead animals.

A deadly brew

By the early 1800s the river was like an open sewer, yet most Londoners still took their drinking water straight from it. Although people complained about the taste of the water, no one realised that it carried deadly diseases, such as typhoid and cholera. From the 1830s onwards, outbreaks of cholera raged throughout London. In the hot summer of 1858, the stench from the river banks became so bad that Members of Parliament ran gagging from Westminster. It finally drove them to deal with the problem.

Waste Away

Until the 1800s, human waste either ended up in the open drains that ran through London's streets, or it was collected in a covered cesspit in the garden or yard. At night the stinking pits were cleared out by gangs of night-soil men.

Then the flush lavatory arrived. It was a wonderful invention. Not only did it wash human waste away quickly and cleanly, it did away with the smelly cesspit, too. By the 1850s, everyone who could afford it was flushing happily. The problem was, everything they flushed away was washed straight into the Thames.

1863
THE FIRST UNDERGROUND TRAIN GOES INTO SERVICE

1864
CHARING CROSS STATION OPENS

1865
THE METROPOLITAN FIRE BRIGADE IS SET UP

Cleaning up

There are almost 100 kinds of fish in the Thames today, including herring, sprat, dace, Dover sole, salmon and flounder.

Using the Thames as a rubbish dump was brought to a halt, and more than 130 kilometres of sewer pipes were built to carry London's waste far downstream to the Thames estuary. Also, by 1870, the cause of cholera had been identified, and water companies were forced to take their supplies from further up the Thames and filter it before selling it.

Today, the Thames in central London is clean enough for fish to swim in it again, and no one complains of the smell.

The big smoke

Londoners were used to the thick, choking brew of coal smoke and fog that lay over the city every winter. They even gave it a name — smog. Throughout the 1800s and early 1900s, many people died from throat and chest infections such as bronchitis and whooping cough.

In December 1952, cold weather and no wind cooked up a real killer of a smog. As many as 4,000 old people and babies died.

Four years later a law was passed called the Clean Air Act. It banned the burning of smoky fuels in London. Nowadays, no one has to rely on coal to heat their home any more and smog is a thing of the past.

London smogs were also called 'pea-soupers'. They made the sky dark in the middle of the day and it was sometimes impossible to see more than a metre ahead.

1866
CANNON STREET STATION IS BUILT IN THE CITY

1868
ST PANCRAS RAILWAY STATION OPENS

1871
THE ALBERT HALL OPENS FOR PUBLIC CONCERTS

You'd be surprised to see a horse in Oxford Street today, but 100 years ago, this busy shopping street was clogged with horses pulling cabs, carts, buses, vans and trams.

About a quarter of a million horses worked on London's roads in 1880. The clatter of hooves and creak of wheels was incredibly noisy. But that wasn't all. Every horse left 3 to 4 tonnes of dung behind it each year!

Over and Under

Until the 1800s, most people got around London on foot. Or, if you could afford it, you could travel by boat, by horse and carriage, or on horseback. This is the way it was for centuries. Then public transport came along.

London's familiar red buses first appeared in 1907, when one of the transport companies of the time painted its buses bright red from roof to wheels.

All together now

In 1829, a group of people hitched a team of horses to a covered coach fitted with 18 seats. They drove their bright idea on a regular route along Marylebone Road and called it an omnibus. The word means 'for all' in Latin, and before long there were lots of horse-drawn buses about.

In 1897, a petrol-engine bus began running from south of the river to Victoria. The effect on horse-drawn buses was devastating. A petrol bus was expensive to buy, but it could carry more passengers over a greater distance — and it didn't need to be stabled or fed! In August 1916, the last horse-drawn bus went out of service.

1873
THE ALBERT
BRIDGE IS BUILT

1874
LIVERPOOL
STREET RAILWAY
STATION OPENS

1879
ELECTRIC STREET
LIGHTING IS USED
ALONG THE
EMBANKMENT

Steaming along

The first railway line in London was built in 1836 and ran from London Bridge to Deptford and Greenwich. Soon, there were railway lines stretching right across the country, and the new railway companies raced each other to build grand stations as close to the centre of London as possible. By 1870, a dozen stations ringed London.

Tunnelling through

In 1837, the journey from Edinburgh to central London took 2 days by stagecoach. Today, an express train does it in 4 hours and 15 minutes.

When the world's first underground steam train travelled from Paddington to the City, in 1863, it was a huge success. It was much quicker than road travel and the fares were reasonable, too.

At first, the tunnels were dug from above, like big ditches, and then covered over. But later, a way of digging out tube-like tunnels from beneath the ground was developed. In 1890, the first of these 'tube' tunnels opened and electric trains ran along it. Soon, tube trains were running all through central London. They were fast and clean, and Londoners loved them.

Today, London's tube trains travel on 392 kilometres of track — almost the same distance as from London to Paris.

What a Story!

London's buses and tubes carry 2.5 million passengers every day, and travel a distance greater than 20 times around the world. In fact, London's transport is so important it even has its own museum.

The **LONDON TRANSPORT MUSEUM** tells the whole story of public transport since 1829. You can see a horse-drawn omnibus, and explore trams, trolley buses and early underground trains.

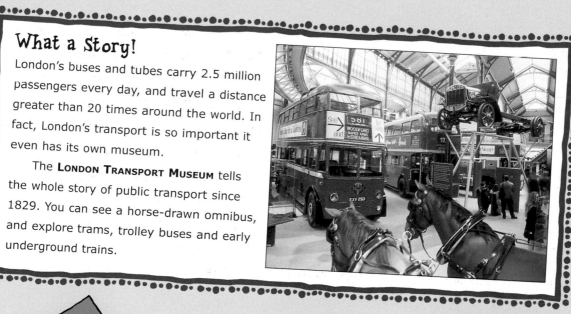

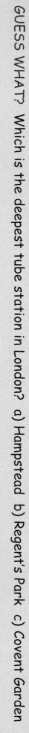

GUESS WHAT? Which is the deepest tube station in London? a) Hampstead b) Regent's Park c) Covent Garden

1881
THE NATURAL HISTORY MUSEUM OPENS IN SOUTH KENSINGTON

1882
THE ROYAL COURTS OF JUSTICE IN THE STRAND ARE COMPLETED

1890
THE FIRST 'TUBE' LINE, THE NORTHERN LINE, OPENS

Putting on a Show

The first playhouse in London was built in 1576. It was very popular, and soon there were lots of theatres competing with each other. They hired writers to churn out a steady stream of new plays. Some of these playwrights are now world-famous names, such as Christopher Marlowe and William Shakespeare.

Going to the theatre became a firm part of London life and today London is one of the great theatre capitals of the world. It has more than 50 theatres in the West End alone, and people travel here from all over the world to enjoy plays, musicals, opera and dance events of all kinds.

SOUTHWARK CATHEDRAL has a monument to Shakespeare inside it to remind us that he first wrote and staged many of his 37 plays nearby.

Playing Around

The original **GLOBE THEATRE** was built in 1599. Most of William Shakespeare's plays were written for the Globe (probably because he owned a share in it).

Like many theatres of the time, the Globe's stage was in the open air. The audience could stand around it in an area known as the yard. Around the yard were three tiers of galleries, covered with a thatched roof. People sat in the galleries on wooden seats.

Plays were performed in the afternoon. The entry price was one penny in the yard, and two or three pence in the galleries.

During a performance in 1613, the thatched roof caught fire and the Globe burned down. In the 1990s, the theatre was rebuilt to match the original as closely as possible, and now Shakespeare's plays are performed at the Globe once again.

Back stage

Galleries

Stage

Yard

1894
TOWER BRIDGE IS COMPLETED

1897
FIRST PETROL-ENGINE BUSES GO INTO SERVICE

1909
SELFRIDGES DEPARTMENT STORE OPENS IN OXFORD STREET

A City of Treasures

Theatres aren't the only places in London that put on wonderful shows for the public. There are art galleries and museums galore as well.

Many of them contain famous treasures from all around the world. Others are not quite so famous, but are still great fun to visit. Here are just a few of them.

The **BRITISH MUSEUM** has so many rooms and so much to see that it's easy to get lost! Check out the Egyptian mummies.

The only painting of Shakespeare that was done while he was alive is inside the **NATIONAL PORTRAIT GALLERY**. See how many other famous people you can spot!

The **NATURAL HISTORY MUSEUM** is an explorer's delight. Don't miss the dinosaurs — or the life-size model of a blue whale!

The **SCIENCE MUSEUM** (right next door to the Natural History Museum) is packed with every invention you can imagine — from steam engines to spacesuits.

If you like ships you'll be able to see lots of them at the **NATIONAL MARITIME MUSEUM**, and find out about the history of the Royal Navy.

And, if you want to see the whole of London's history under one roof, the only place to go is the **MUSEUM OF LONDON**.

GUESS WHAT? Which is the oldest museum in London? a) the Victoria & Albert b) Pollock's Toy Museum c) the British Museum

1940
BOMBING RAIDS BEGIN ON LONDON

1945
WORLD WAR II ENDS. ONE THIRD OF LONDON'S BUILDINGS LIE IN RUINS

2000
LONDON CELEBRATES A NEW MILLENNIUM

London Today

At the start of a new millennium, London is still one of the greatest cities in the world.

How much of a 'Londoner' are you? Here's a list of the places you've read about in this book. Tick the box if you've been there; then see how many answers in our London Quiz you can get right.

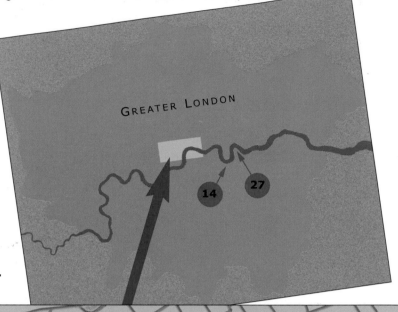

GREATER LONDON

14 27

A **Tower Bridge**
B **London Bridge**
C **Southwark Bridge**
D **Millennium Bridge**
E **Blackfriars Bridge**
F **Waterloo Bridge**
G **Westminster Bridge**
H **Lambeth Bridge**

TOTTENHAM COURT ROAD

HIGH HOLBORN

2

REGENT STREET

CHARING CROSS ROAD

OXFORD STREET

18

11

4 10

STRAND

15

HYDE PARK

VICTORIA EMBANKMENT

F

PICCADILLY

GREEN PARK

20 THE MALL

1

ST. JAMES PARK

G

3

BROMPTON ROAD

26 8

23

VICTORIA STREET

19

H

9

16

1 **The Banqueting House** was once part of a palace. Was it: a) St James's, b) Lambeth, c) Whitehall?

2 The **British Museum** is in: a) Bloomsbury, b) Chelsea, c) Battersea.

3 When the Queen is at **Buckingham Palace** a flag flies from: a) the balcony, b) the gate, c) the roof.

4 Originally, **Covent Garden** was: a) a fun-fair, b) a vegetable patch, c) a rose garden.

5 **Custom House** is the headquarters of: a) fire-fighters, b) ferry boatmen, c) tax collectors.

6 The **Globe Theatre** is famous for its special shape. Is it: a) doughnut-shaped, b) triangular, c) pear-shaped?

7 **Goldsmiths' Hall** is: a) a building made of gold, b) where members of the Goldsmiths' Guild meet, c) a concert hall.

8 The **Houses of Parliament (Palace of Westminster)** has a famous bell hanging in it called: a) Long John, b) Big Bertha, c) Big Ben.

9 **Lambeth Palace** is the home of the: a) Bishop of Winchester, b) Archbishop of Canterbury, c) Archbishop of York.

10 At the **London Transport Museum** you can operate the controls of: a) an underground train, b) an aeroplane, c) a river boat.

11 At **Marble Arch** there is a marker for the: a) Tyburn Tree, b) Shepherd's Bush, c) Golder's Green.

15 The **National Portrait Gallery** contains famous paintings of: a) landscapes, b) buildings, c) people.

16 The **Natural History Museum** has a model of the heaviest animal that has ever lived. Is it a: a) blue whale, b) *Brachiosaurus*, c) giant squid?

17 If you are sent to the **Old Bailey** you will see: a) a play, b) a doctor, c) a judge.

18 The **Royal Courts of Justice** are on: a) Oxford Street, b) The Strand, c) Whitehall.

19 In the entrance to the **Science Museum** you can see the wheels of: a) a jumbo jet, b) a space rocket, c) a submarine.

20 **St James's Palace** was built by: a) Henry VIII, b) William the Conqueror, c) Edward the Confessor.

21 What kinds of boats are moored at **St Katharine Dock** today? a) warships, b) yachts, c) rowing boats?

22 The present **St Paul's Cathedral** was built by: a) Christopher Sparrow, b) Christopher Robin, c) Christopher Wren.

23 **St Thomas' Hospital** was founded by: a) monks, b) soldiers, c) shopkeepers.

24 In **Southwark Cathedral** there is a monument to: a) William Tell, b) William Shakespeare, c) William of Orange.

25 The famous birds that live at the **Tower of London** are: a) swans, b) ravens, c) pigeons.

26 **Westminster Abbey** as we know it today was built by: a) Henry VIII, b) Henry VI, c) Henry III.

12 The **Monument** is a memorial to the: a) Great Fire, b) Great Plague, c) Great Stink.

13 At the **Museum of London** you can see a piece of a Roman: a) bath, b) bridge, c) wall.

14 The **National Maritime Museum** is in: a) Bermondsey, b) Greenwich, c) Blackheath.

27 The **Millennium Dome** at Greenwich was built to celebrate: a) the past 100 years, b) the past 1,000 years, c) the past 1,000,000 years?

Index

Quiz Answers

PAGE 5: b) & c) There are 18 road bridges, but if you add 2 footbridges (including the new Millennium Bridge) and 8 railway bridges that makes 28 in all.

PAGE 7: b) There have been 38 coronations in Westminster Abbey. The two kings that weren't crowned there are Edward V and Edward VIII.

PAGE 9: c) There are 3 km of corridors in the Houses of Parliament, and over 1,000 rooms for MPs and their staff.

PAGE 11: b) There are 44 churches in the City of London.

PAGE 13: c) In 1941, Josef Jakobs was executed in the Tower for spying against England in World War II. He was shot. The last person to be beheaded in England was in 1746.

PAGE 15: a) HMS *Belfast* is the biggest.

PAGE 19: b) The Cordwainers' Guild made shoes. The Cutlers made knives and the Coopers made wooden barrels.

PAGE 21: b) The true cause of the plague is the germ *yersinia pestis*, and it was discovered by doctors working in India in 1907.

PAGE 23: b) At the last count (taken in 1997) London's population was 7,122,000.

PAGE 25: a) Most of London's drinking water comes from huge reservoirs fed by the Thames.

PAGE 27: a) Hampstead is the deepest tube station in London. It is 58.5 metres below ground.

PAGE 29: c) The British Museum is the oldest museum in London. It first opened in 1759 in a house in Bloomsbury, and in 1847 it moved into its present building.

PAGES 30–31:
1c; 2a; 3c; 4b; 5c; 6a; 7b; 8c; 9b; 10a; 11a; 12a; 13c; 14b; 15c; 16a; 17c; 18b; 19a; 20a; 21b; 22c; 23a; 24b; 25b; 26c; 27b.